His Adventure Begins

by Lucy Rosen

Screenplay by
Marc Haimes and Chris Butler

Story by
Shannon Tindle and Marc Haimes

LITTLE, BROWN & COMPANY
LB kids

Little, Brown and Company

Hachette Book Group
1290 Avenue of the Americas, New York, NY 10104
Visit our website at lb-kids.com

Little, Brown and Company is a division of Hachette Book Group, Inc.
The Little, Brown name and logo are trademarks of Hachette Book Group, Inc.

The publisher is not responsible for websites (or their content) that are not owned by the publisher.

First Edition: July 2016

Library of Congress Control Number: 2016938207

ISBN 978-0-316-36140-8

10 9 8 7 6 5 4 3 2 1

CW

Printed in the United States of America

This is Kubo. Look at him closely. What do you see? You may notice his serious expression or the *shamisen* he carries on his back. You may even notice that Kubo wears an eye patch.

What you can't see at first glance is Kubo's magic gift. Only those brave enough to join him on his journey can see what makes his story so special.

Our hero may look like an ordinary boy, but his tale is one unlike any other.

Long before Kubo was born, his mother belonged to
a magical family. Her father was the evil Moon King—
the ruler of all that is cold, dark, and lonely.

Then one day, Kubo's mother met the mighty warrior Hanzo. And although they came from different worlds, the two soon fell in love.

When the Moon King discovered that his daughter had chosen a new
life alongside his enemies, he swore revenge. And after Kubo was born, his
parents knew it was only a matter of time before the Moon King attacked.
While Hanzo was fighting, Kubo's mother fled with their son to safety
on the sea.

Now Kubo is a young boy. He lives with his mother in a hidden cave, tucked away on the edge of a small village. During the day, he roams the streets and performs his magic for the villagers.

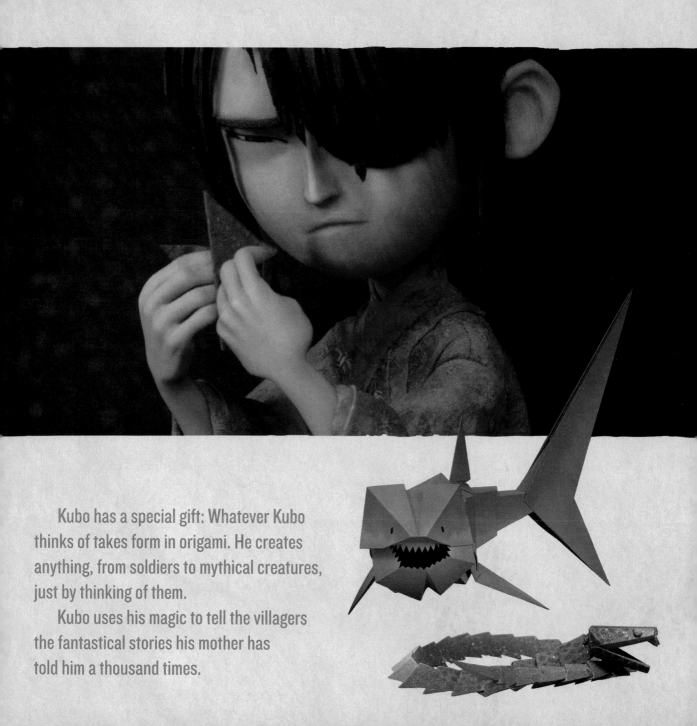

Kubo has a special gift: Whatever Kubo thinks of takes form in origami. He creates anything, from soldiers to mythical creatures, just by thinking of them.

Kubo uses his magic to tell the villagers the fantastical stories his mother has told him a thousand times.

Kubo's favorite story is of Hanzo's quest for a magic set of armor. It was the only thing in the whole world that could protect him from the power of the Moon King!

This armor was made up of three pieces: the Sword Unbreakable, the Breastplate Impenetrable, and the Helmet Invulnerable!

The villagers cheer as they watch a tiny paper Hanzo set off on his mission, surrounded by hundreds of origami creations that Kubo has brought to life.

Every day, Kubo tells another chapter in the saga of Hanzo and the Moon King. And every day, his mother worries that the Moon King and her terrible sisters will find them.

Late at night, Kubo is awakened by the fluttering of wings and the skittering of paper. Like Kubo, his mother's dreams come to life as origami—except for her, they are always nightmares.

One day, Kubo hears some villagers talking about an ancient ritual using lamps and altars to speak with generations of ancestors.

Kubo can't believe his ears. "You mean, you can talk to the dead?" he asks.

"Yes," say the villagers. "Is there someone you'd like to speak with?"

Kubo thinks of Hanzo, his father. "Very much," he says.

Kubo follows the villagers deep into the woods. He waits and waits for a word from his father, but nothing comes.

Behind him, the sun begins to set.
Kubo has lost track of time!

A dark shadow unfurls across the sky, stamping out every remaining trace of light. Kubo hears his name in the air: *"Kuuuuuubo! Kuuuuubooooo!"* He follows the sound of these whispered voices.

Two women stand across the river, wearing black robes that billow in the breeze. "Come, Kubo," they beckon. "Come to your aunties."

Kubo gasps as he realizes what has happened. He has stayed out too late, and now the Two Sisters have found him!

Kubo runs as fast as he can toward the village. The Two Sisters follow closely behind.

"No reason to be afraid," they call after him, their awful voices frosty and sharp.

The boy is no match for The Sisters' powerful magic, and soon he has nowhere left to run. Kubo braces for the icy grip of The Sisters' hands.

But it never comes. Before The Sisters are able to grab him, Kubo's mother leaps out of nowhere and sends them flying!

"Kubo, you must find your father's armor! It's your only chance!" his mother cries. She places a magic beetle crest on the back of his robe. Two wings spring out, flapping furiously and lifting Kubo into the air, carrying him far away.

Kubo wakes up in a snowbank. When he opens his eye,
all he can see is snow...and a monkey.

"I'm here to protect you," says Monkey.

Kubo's mother has sent him to follow in the warrior Hanzo's footsteps, searching for the magic suit of armor that will protect him against the Moon King.

Kubo and Monkey set off. Soon, they encounter Beetle, a strange creature who is convinced he knows Kubo from somewhere.

They soon discover Beetle knew Kubo's father! This must be a
sign that their mission is taking shape. But Monkey isn't so sure.
She doesn't trust Beetle...but she also knows that they can use all
the help they can get.

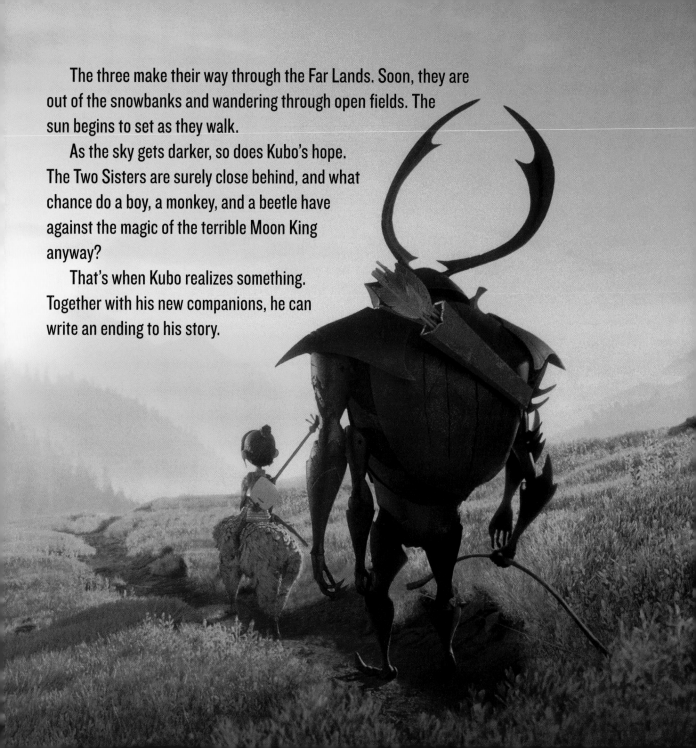

The three make their way through the Far Lands. Soon, they are out of the snowbanks and wandering through open fields. The sun begins to set as they walk.

As the sky gets darker, so does Kubo's hope. The Two Sisters are surely close behind, and what chance do a boy, a monkey, and a beetle have against the magic of the terrible Moon King anyway?

That's when Kubo realizes something. Together with his new companions, he can write an ending to his story.